PERFECT
IMPERFECTIONS

About The Author

Prosper Wilton Makara is a Zimbabwean male in his twenties who loves reading and writing. He is obsessed by Nigerian writer Chimamanda Ngozi Adichie, the author of Americanah.

Also By The Same Author

CRUSHED DESIRE: Short Stories Collection

PERFECT IMPERFECTIONS

PROSPER WILTON MAKARA

Darling Kind Publishing

An Imprint of TatendaCharlesMunyuki Publishing

PERFECT IMPERFECTIONS

First published in Zimbabwe in 2017
Darling Kind Publishing
an imprint of Tatenda Charles Munyuki Publishing

Copyright © Prosper Wilton Makara 2017
Cover Illustration Copyright© Straightline Designz 2017
Cover illustration by Straightline Designz 2017

The moral rights of the author have been asserted.

ISBN   978 0 7974 7889 3

Printed and bound by Darling Kind Publishing,
Harare, Zimbabwe.
darlingkindp@live.com

facebook.com/tcmpublishingzim

ACKNOWLEDGEMENTS

My deepest gratitude to you Rumbidzai Masvaure for being a true pillar and supporting me whenever I lost hope. Thank you for always saying, 'You can,' whenever I needed to hear it and for your strange unwavering support. Nicholas, for helping refresh my mind from time to time as I worked on my book.

I would not forget my family especially Professor Brighton, my young brother for your excellence and remarkable generosity in reading my manuscript, more than once and letting me see my characters through their eyes.

I'm forever grateful.

Prosper W. Makara 2017

This book is to my mother, in whom I have found comfort and true love.
Also to Nicholas, a special friend and as always to you Rumbidzai.

Rumbidzai had grown up to be a very beautiful and intelligent young woman. By the age of eighteen, she had finished her Advanced Level studies and had done extremely well. She had worked very hard in school, studying during the night by candlelight. She would help with the chores before she left for school. All along, her ambition had been to be a successful lawyer, but now she was seeing a bleak end to her supposedly bright future. Her father had died when she was in form two and her mother's meagre earnings couldn't manage to cater for her university funds. Mai Dengu didn't have a steady job, but did odd jobs at people's homesteads. Her work-gnarled hands bore witness to her hard work. Due to these financial challenges, Rumbidzai had married early to a young teacher who taught at the local school. Both, because she wanted to alleviate her mother's suffering and because that was now the noblest thing to do since she was now an unemployed young woman without anything better to do than to play housewife.

Tafara and Rumbidzai had been the kind of lovebirds that were inseparable. You could never spot either far from the other. They both had characters to be envied. Rumbidzai had been the kind of girl who was reserved and faithful.

Their family was growing now and her husband was due to be transferred to the city. It seemed all things were indeed working for the good. Her first-born son was only a year old and she was expecting another baby. This child was to be born in Salisbury for, by then Tafara would have already been transferred. She had never set eyes on the City though she had heard much of its magic from Sekuru Tanga. He claimed to have worked as a garden boy at a white man's house, a claim that no one ever confirmed as true.

'*Aah iwe. Muzukuru, ndakashanda pamurungu muHarare nguva refu ini. Takanetsa padhoroba. Vaitotizeza, kutozodzoka kumusha ndaona kuti ndachembera,*' he would say in his funny monotonous voice.

She laughed as she dismissed the thoughts of her funny uncle to that of her young husband.

***

'Have you already prepared your field for the coming rain season, my daughter?' Mai Dengu asked sitting cross-legged on the cracked floor all the while peering into the pot by the fire in which she was preparing her lunch.

'I have dug, Amai, but it took me unusually long this time. You know how your grandchild Timothy wants undivided attention. He is such a troublesome child,' she answered steadying the door by a brick for its hinges were making an irritating noise.

'The poor child was dumped by his father before he was not even weaned,' Mai Dengu said as though it was the reason for her son's restlessness. This conversation was turning familiar. Her mother always found the tiniest of excuses to criticizing the absence of Tafara in their lives.

'Please, mother, not now!' Rumbidzai snapped. Her anger was unmistakable.

'What is it, my child?' Mai Dengu asked, speaking almost to herself still somewhat shocked by her daughter's uncustomary anger.

'Mother, how can you speak evil against Tafara?' Rumbi asked with a choked voice.

'My daughter, can't you see the tough times Tafara is putting you through? Bringing up a child on your own is hard work. I am only acting as a concerned mother with your best interests at heart. Look, you have almost neglected self-grooming due to the hard work you are doing on your own to keep afloat. The job you are doing is ageing you and you almost look as old as your mother. If he was here, he would have helped,' her mother said attending to her pot. When she replaced the lid of the pot, she then began putting some firewood into the fire, which was now dying out.

'He did not abandon me, Amai,' Rumbidzai remained adamant. 'You are making it sound as if he divorced me or something. We both know he had our best interest at heart when he left for South Africa. He wanted a better job that would bring in more money for his family. No matter what you say, I know that he will be back to...'

'Don't be so naïve, Rumbidzai. Has he ever communicated since his departure? No. But you want to wait all the same, *unoda kuita Garandichauya*? Surely, the one who bewitched you is dead my daughter. You should be thinking like a grown up. What if he has already met a new woman? Would he still remember his village girl after he finds a town girl? What if he is already dead?' Her mother was now speaking with a raised voice and Rumbidzai knew better than to stop her before she had finished speaking.

This was the height of the colonial era. She understood her mother's concern. The possibility of Tafara's death was not entirely dismissive although she didn't want to believe so. She knew that she would never reach an understanding with her mother, so she decided to let the issue pass. There was a moment of silence. Rumbidzai had something to say, but she could not find the right way to put it.

'The headmaster came to my house yesterday Amai and he had some news for me,' she finally said.

'You mean the headmaster from the high school?' Her mother said all too curious to know every detail.

'Yes, mother.'

'What did he have to say?' Mai Dengu was now giving undivided attention to what Rumbidzai had to say.

'The USAID organization has finally responded to my scholarship application. They have said I am no doubt a stellar student and they have offered me a scholarship to study at Cambridge University,' she said without showing her current standpoint on the subject. She wasn't showing any sign of excitement.

'That's wonderful news, my daughter. The Lord has surely remembered us this time,' her mother's elation on hearing the news was unmistakable.

'Mother, don't tell me you are expecting me to go? I have a very young child and I'm still pregnant.

After all, I'm now married,' she said laughing

'What do you mean, Rumbidzai? Aren't you the one who always wanted to be a lawyer? What's new in having a child and being married? Married to a man who has left you for months now without any communication? My advice is that you go and finish your studies then you will have a good job and be able to take good care of yourself,' Mai Dengu said as she began to dish out food into the plates.

'Mother, what about my unborn baby? I can't study overseas whilst I'm still expecting?'

'Rumbidzai, don't be like a child, my daughter! I say you terminate it, visit the Sangoma and...'

'What do you mean terminate it, mother? That's an unpardonable sin,' Rumbidzai shot back instantaneously, repulsed by her mother's line of thought.

'You heard me well, my daughter. You should terminate the pregnancy. Chances like these do not come by every day. You can have as many children as you want after your studies. You are no longer a child my dear. Go out there, study hard and find a new and better man who can take good care of us.'

Rumbidzai had been infuriated by her inconsiderate mother's short sightedness. Her words had stung her. *How could she easily forget all Tafara had done for their family?* Tears fell freely on her face. How could her mother be cold and frigid like this? Was it possible that there was some truth in what her mother was saying? She didn't even want to imagine aborting her unborn baby. After a long argument with her mother, Mai Dengu closed the discussion saying, 'Do as I say, I am your mother and I know what's best for you.' After saying this, she had stormed out of the room not caring for an answer from Rumbidzai. Rumbidzai cried all day long about it.

It was then she had learnt to be strong.

Had it not been for the phone call, Rochelle would have spent the rest of her day in very high spirits. Coiled deep inside her was an inkling feeling that something was terribly wrong. It had only been a few frantic words exchanged, but they had been enough to awaken something dark and glum inside her.

She hadn't even noticed that she was crying until she felt a warm droplet fall on her favourite silk night dress. It was then she started wiping the tears off. She wanted to believe that she was overreacting. There was probably no problem back home. She desperately wanted to believe that, but she failed even to convince herself. She had always been intuitive even as a child and her family knew it.

She sat on the edge of the bed and shook Trevor. Her sweetheart. Her high school crush. They had married soon after their graduation. Although it had felt like rushing things, nobody had complained. Everyone knew that Trevor adored Rochelle and would never hurt her, just like the latter was devoted to the former. Theirs was a perfect relationship without any mishaps. Rochelle and Trevor in their thirties were both intelligent lawyers at adversary law firms. Both of their bosses seriously considered making them partners.

Despite their tight work schedules, they always squeezed time for their romantic getaways.

Their love and commitment was almost too

much, if that was possible. One day, a week before their marriage, they had visited Rochelle's parents at Chishawasha Hills. Being *part psychic* as she was, she had noticed that her mother wanted to talk to her about something, but didn't know how.

'Rochelle my dear,' her mother had finally said when Trevor had gone out with Rochelle's father. 'You love Trevor,' she smiled and kept quiet. That wasn't a question so Rochelle didn't feel mandated to say anything. 'I think you love him more than necessary.'

Rochelle sighed and took a small sip of her drink thinking of the best possible way to respond to her mother.

'I have never seen anything like you guys have before. It's in the way he looks at you. He stares at you all the time, practically leaning towards you like he is about to jump in front of a bullet for you. But then, that isn't all. Whenever Trevor shifts his position, you also unconsciously shift to keep in close alignment with him. It's like you are some kind of magnets that draw together. I don't know. It's very hard to explain.'

'Oh, Mom,' Rochelle had said sounding exasperated. 'Have you been reading sci-fi novels or what?'

'No, my dear, I stick to Mills and Boon. I just want you to be careful Rochelle. I love you.'

She knew her mother was a pretty woman. That bothered her very much. Women were supposed to be strong.

Trevor was awakened by a gentle nudge from Rochelle. Rochelle had the look of someone who was lost in thought. This always gave Trevor an almost desperate, dire desire to soothe her. 'Why are you crying my love?' He asked with a low calming voice.

'I know this is stupid and I'm blowing things out of proportion Trevor. It's just a phone call that got me worried sick,' Rochelle became hysterical after saying this, choking and gulping for air.

Trevor let her cry whilst coaxing her with his arms. 'You are not stupid. You are an intelligent and loving lady,' he murmured. 'Tell me about it. Tell me about the phone call.'

Rochelle sighed and adjusted her head on Trevor's chest. 'I was just finishing my research for that rape case when the phone rang. It was mother.'

She told him all about the phone call that was making her lose her marbles. How her mother had a hoarse voice, supposedly from crying, and seemed to be on the verge of crying. She also tried to explain to him how she had known that something terrible had happened. She knew and she was definite that it was death. That night as she tossed and turned in her bed trying to sleep, she recalled her mother's words on the phone, *You have to come, forget about work this time, my life has crumbled down, it is all crumbling down.*

ENGLAND, CAMBRIDGE
CAMBRIDGE UNIVERSITY, 1977

Hugh Truman had grown up as a well-matured boy, maybe a bit mature for his age. He was a quiet boy who kept to himself. Even at school, he hardly associated with other students. This was mostly because his family had moved from Australia when he was only five years of age and beginning to make a social circle.

In Zimbabwe, he found the environment very different from what he was used to. In Australia, they had lived in the outback of Belvedere. Children were always running all about in the open. He had had no trouble interacting back then.

Now their life in Chishawasha Hills was altogether different. At no time would you find people having an idle chat in the streets. People left and arrived in their cars, moreover their houses were far apart, you could live in this suburb for some time without meeting your neighbour. Wanting the best from her last-born child, Mrs Truman had had Hugh home-schooled up to Advanced level. He had done extremely well and was set to study Law at Cambridge University. His mother reasoned that this was just the exposure he needed to kick-start a new law firm with an exceptionally good reputation. Being a single parent, his mother was strong willed and she wanted the best for her children. At Cambridge, she had arranged that Hugh would stay with her brother, Lucas. She knew quite well that Hugh wouldn't be comfortable in the campus residence nor was he going to be comfortable at sharing his stuff.

When he had gone to school, Hugh kept to himself. He found no amusement in the boisterous spirits of his fellow classmates. Just like himself, there was a girl who was highly reserved in his class.

Though the lady was African, she was a stellar student like him. There was however not a point when doubt had arisen, that the lady was the best student in the class.

The young lady was a natural beauty with silky skin. She hardly wore any makeup, but cheap lip-gloss and lotion.

Her eyes held a sad look, even when she smiled you could see that in her eyes was written a story of pain and hurt. She was slender and her figure wasn't quite voluptuous, but she had an undeniable charm and was attractive all the same. Hugh admired her beauty in simplicity.

Tracy had been the awfully shy kind of girl- not like Eileen who had openly told him that she wanted him to have sex with her even though they were not dating or Lorraine the Jamaican girl who always rolled her buttocks ridiculously when she passed by him.

She was one of the three African students in the Law class at Cambridge. What always amazed Hugh about Tracy was her ability to gain confidence in the law arena. In classroom, she was the confident lady who won any scholarly debate. Her professors had noticed her unusual brilliance and had developed a genuine liking to her. She was generally enthused by law studies and always excelled, but never at any point did she cease being humble. Maybe her enthusiasm and insatiable scramble for information was in part because where she came from education was bottlenecked and a privilege for the elite class. He couldn't tell.

On one occasion, they had been studying about the equality of the races and in the midst of a vehement debate Tracy had stood up and made a speech. She had spoken boldly in the huge lecture theatre silencing the ongoing pandemonium. The professor and all students had given her a standing ovation. That's when Hugh finally came to the conclusion of his devious plan. He was to have this girl. He wanted her to himself. To marry her. To use her to get money. Tracy was intelligent and there was no doubt she could help set out a reputable law firm. He concluded this as he listened to Tracy's last part of the speech.

'...It baffles me. Why are we termed black? I wonder if there is really any one black. No, I refuse to be called black for I know that I am peanut butter brown, the colour of sweetness. I am a proud piece of chocolate brown. Yes, I am an African Child. We were deprived of education by those who called themselves *helpers*. Us being called *guerrillas*, people of low IQ by those who thought knew better. My mother's language they deemed lame. English and a bit of French were tamer. When we protested, they massacred. They left me puzzled, dazzled and muddled. I was like a crushed flower in the fields barren, a flickering light in darkness dense. I am an African Child! Not a candidate to isolation. Though a victim to sneers, I refute all claims of self-pity. Arise with me African children. Let us take the bull by its horns and take charge of our future. I know I can, I know you can and I know we can. Know that the best way out is always through. For to die and err is human, but life is divine. Africa is my motherland. Victory is what I am gunning for, as an African Child.'

ZIMBABWE, HARARE
BAINES HOSPITAL, 2016

Rutendo had been working the night shift when she received the call. As soon as she put the receiver down, she realized that she had cool beads of perspiration on her forehead. She found herself shivering despite the warm temperatures set by the air conditioner. Rutendo took very deep breaths to help calm her down. 'Calm down. Calm down. Calm down.'

Her brain was screaming, but her subconscious was telling her otherwise. Deep down within her she knew that something was wrong. An inkling feeling was yelling for her attention. It was certain that a gloomy future loomed. But she had to calm down. She had to be professional and end her shift. She was a professional ophthalmologist.

Rutendo was a goal oriented young woman. In her early thirties, she had already built an empire for herself. A specialization in Ophthalmology was a guarantee of serious money on her table.

Her uncle had once teased her saying that no man in his right mind would want her for a wife if she kept on amassing wealth. The chair of the department of Ophthalmology at the hospital had asked if she wasn't worried that men would be intimidated by her. With all she had acquired. She was only in her mid-twenties by then, but with all the pride she could master and head held high, she said she wouldn't. She hadn't worried. In fact, it had not occurred to her to worry.

The men who would be intimidated by her were exactly the kind she wouldn't want.

It was two years later when she had finally met Felix. By then her parents were already worried by their spinster child although they hadn't mentioned it to her. Rutendo had liked him instantly.

How couldn't she? He had just the right kind of humour, warmth and charm. Not too much of any quality. They fell in love in winter and married on the onset of summer. They were adults who were certain of what they wanted. At thirty, she had two children a year apart. Both, lovely and adorable girls.

It was then, when she gave birth to the children, his children, that their old flame extinguished. Although Rutendo had suspected that Felix was cheating on her, she had never had substantial evidence. But then, all the signs were there. He started coming back home late and leaving very early. It seemed he was outside the house more than he was in. He even started having mysterious management meetings, on weekends. And whenever he came from these meetings he oozed of ecstatic energy and happiness, wearing a smug expression of one who had a mischievous plan up their sleeve. He forgot the dates for their anniversary and her birthday. He changed his wardrobe and social circle.

Felix was definitely cheating on Rutendo.

Their relationship had changed for the worst. The way they interacted was affected as he became moody, grouchy and dispassionate in the extreme.

A text message from Rochelle brought Rutendo back to her senses.

Have you received the call?

This meant that probably every one of her siblings had received the bizarre call. She quickly responded.

Yes. I'm scared.

The reply came only moments later.

So am I. Something is wrong.

Rochelle was never wrong. Her gut feeling was always correct. At one point in time, she had freaked everyone when an accident was being reported on television and she had suddenly said, 'Oh my God! Gogo was in that bus.' They had received a call from the police five minutes later alerting them of the death of Gogo.

Rutendo hadn't noticed that she was moving until she came face to face with her supervisor. She asked him to excuse her for the rest of the night to which he obliged very willingly. He had always been infatuated by her. He didn't mind the number of times he was turned down - he claimed to be patient.

Felix was not at home, as usual. These days he rarely was home. Rutendo picked a note that was on the table. It was written in elegant and confident strokes. *I will be home late.*

Coming from Felix that meant more likely like, 'Hey, Rutendo! I won't be coming home today.'

She sighed. She had to appreciate that this was

probably the nicest gesture Felix had made in a long time. 'All will be well soon,' she tried to comfort herself. Sadly, she couldn't convince herself.

Rutendo hurried to the bedroom to have a change of clothes. She was running late. Whatever news awaited her, good or bad, she had to hurry.

She didn't know why, but disturbingly grotesque images of her mother lying dead and nearly disfigured kept floating in her eyes. She didn't want to dwell on the gore. She was scared beyond her wits. Scared that possibly the nightmares she had been having for the past month would come true. She was frightened that she couldn't handle a death. Especially her mother's death. Emily, her friend who happened to be a psychiatrist at the same hospital she worked for had said that these were probably side effects of an abusive relationship.

Oh, how she had wanted to believe Emily, to blame the nightmares on an unsuspecting Felix. She had a sinking feeling that this was not the issue. The dreams were now more vivid and elaborate even though Felix was now only beating her twice a week and never asking for sex more than once in a decade.

Her languorous day had changed. Without even bothering to write a note or text about her whereabouts to Felix, she left. The effort was futile. It was like trying to merge the same poles of a magnet together. She made a mental note that she would give up trying to mend things with Felix. In fact, she was going to file for a divorce. She had to free herself.

UNITED ARAB EMIRATES
DUBAI, 1979

Hugh stood outside the bedroom, which he shared with his new wife, his hand poised as he hesitated, wondering whether after all he would knock on the door. It was the fifth night of their honeymoon and if the last four nights were anything to go by, he could not exactly expect a rapturous welcome.

His wife, he was discovering, possessed an almost fanatical concern for orderliness, and when Hugh climbed into bed beside her, she would not lie back upon her pillow until she had straightened the covers he had disturbed and rearranged the sheet to her satisfaction. As if this was not sufficiently disquieting, she requested him politely not to untie the ribbons on her nightgown as they had only just been ironed by her maid and she did not wish them creased.

Once the light had been turned off, Hugh was permitted to lift the hem of her gown and *do as he pleased* so long as he did not rumple her hair or the bed. She gave no sign that she wished to participate in the act of love and as soon as it was accomplished, she hurried to her bathroom from whence came the vigorous splashing of water, indicating her desire to be cleansed of all evidence of his passion. On her return, she made no reference to the subject and such conversation as ensued, covered her plans for the following day. Intentionally or otherwise, she managed in this manner to make Hugh feel there had been no union at all.

Perhaps the fault is mine, Hugh thought. *Maybe I'm not doing it right.* As she had told him, since she was raped at such a tender age, she had not yet recovered from the trauma. He must try to be more patient, to initiate Tracy slowly and gently into the pleasures that could be theirs.

His wife was in bed. The big room looked warm and inviting in the soft candlelight. Hugh was pleased to see that Tracy had dismissed her day clothing and that like himself, she was already in her night attire. She was sitting in the centre of the large double bed. He walked over and sat beside her.

For a moment, a feeling of bitterness swept over him as he realized that her expression would shortly become one of revulsion when he climbed in beside her.

'You must not be afraid of me, Tracy,' he said softly. 'We are man and wife, and you have nothing to fear from me,' he added, as he blew out the candles. As he slipped into bed and put his hands gently on her shoulders, he felt her body stiffen.

'You are lying on my arm, Hugh,' he heard her whisper in the darkness. Ignoring her protest, he undid the ribbons of her nightgown. As his hand covered her breast, he was aware that although he could see nothing, she was gritting her teeth in horror.

'Would you prefer me not sleeping with you tonight? Perhaps you are tired?' He suggested in a hard tight voice.

There was a moment's hesitation before Tracy said, 'No, you can stay if you want to. I really do not mind, Hugh...' Nevertheless, she edged away, and the lack of welcome in her tone successfully quelled any last vestige of desire he might have felt.

Oh God, he thought, *what in heaven's name am I doing here in bed with a woman I do not want and who most certainly does not want me?* The most sensible thing to do now, he decided, was to excuse himself from a thoroughly uncomfortable situation.

He pretended a deep yawn. 'After all, my dear, on reflection we do have quite a heavy schedule tomorrow. Perhaps it would do us both good to have an early night.'

At once, Tracy's body relaxed and she actually turned her head and kissed his cheek. 'Of course, if you say so, Hugh, I am a little tired, but... well, naturally, dearest, I did not want to disappoint you...'

Knowing that he had no right to be angry since the suggestion had been his, Hugh faced the other side in an unsettled frame of mind. He would be a fool to go on pretending that this side of his marriage would ever prove satisfactory. There were many women who were cold and frigid like Tracy – a fact he had learned from other ladies who had welcomed him to their bed. 'The very reason why many men were unfaithful to their wives,' a certain actress had told him. It was far from uncommon. He did not want his marriage to be lacking in this respect, he told himself.

He had been looking forward to this fortnight in the romantic Dubai, away from home, supposing that he and Tracy would set the foundations for a happy life together. Now he could only hope that when they were back in Harare and Tracy had had time to become more accustomed to her married status, matters would improve.

ZIMBABWE, HARARE
CHISHAWASHA HILLS, 2016

Natsai knocked on the main door to her parents' house. Their home. All the lights were on which was surprising because her parents were always been conservative people. They saved electricity, water, paper, and they even recycled. Stranger still was the fact that nobody was answering the knock.

She pushed the door wide open already panicked by the lack of response. 'Mom! Mhamha, where are you?'

She was the closest to their parents being the last-born. They had that kind of connection, which was why her heart was beating erratically now. She knew it. Something was terribly wrong.

She hurried her way towards her mother's bedroom. It seemed quiet odd that her mother wasn't in the kitchen, her favourite place trying out some wild recipes if not having a casual drink whilst reading a book. The house seemed drained off life. She was suddenly a bit hesitant to take the last few steps to the bedroom, afraid of what she would find there.

She opened the door. She wasn't prepared for the image that met her eyes. Her mother lay sprawled on the floor, her eyes bloated and a shade darker than magenta. Her teeth looked worryingly brittle against the deep red slickness of the lipstick that she wore. Natsai had never seen her mother so brittle. Not in control. Her heart skipped a bit and she shuttered. 'Who did this to you, Amai?'

But even as she asked she knew very well that nobody had hurt her mother. It must have been something to do with fate's rulings. All of a sudden, the gloominess in the room increased. She became increasingly aware of its ominous presence and it was threatening to choke her.

She had to get a firm grip on herself and be there for her mother.

'It's your father. He...he....he is dead.'

Natsai's world came to a dead halt. It felt like all the world's burden was crashing in on her. *Was it possible that her handsome, vibrant and youthful father was dead?* The man she had seen holding that signature contagious exuberance only the previous week had died?

'What do you mean that Baba is dead, Amai? Talk to me!' She was now hyperventilating.

Her mother, her face contorted in pure agony and tears gushing out of her eyes was trying to steady herself by holding to the bed.

'His secretary found him dead in his office this afternoon. Apparently, it was a heart failure. Anyway that's what the hospital said.'

'Come on, Amai, that's ludicrous. How can Dad have a heart failure? He never had a heart problem and he is the most health conscious person I know.'

Natsai would not find out what her mother's response was going to be because at that very moment the front door opened. Rochelle and Rutendo had arrived. Natsai could hear Rochelle calling out for their mother. For the first time ever, Natsai heard her oldest sister trying, but failing miserably, to sound calm.

It was she, Natsai, who had to retell the bad ordeal that had befallen the family to her sisters, their mother obviously couldn't face the pain again. They both were as shocked as they were pained by the news. The news had caught them unaware and made just the right kind of damage. Their father had had a heart failure, as vibrant and health conscious as he was.

It was a pathetic sight. The three sisters crying hysterically. Their mother once again sprawled on the floor. No longer weeping. Apparently, she was out of tears. But it was all in her eyes. Her eyes held all the pain. She had lost her husband. Her source of joy, love, and mutual support.

She was as good as dead.

RHODHESIA,
UMTALI, 1979

Three weeks later, sitting on the sofa in the lounge, Hugh laughed at himself. He recalled that moment of tentative optimism and realized that it was unfounded.

Was it really possible that he was married to this woman? He thought uneasily, as he listened to the scratch of her pen. The words of the wedding ceremony crossed his mind, *love, cherish, worship.* Somehow, they did not seem to apply to his feelings to Tracy.

His thoughts slipped further back to the memory of his bride as she walked up the aisle on the arm of her proud and smiling uncle. The church had been crowded. The colourful attire of their hundreds of fashionable friends added to the festivity of the occasion and momentarily dispelled the depression that had inevitably followed the carousing at his bachelor's party the night before.

His friends had ribbed him unmercifully, calling him a half-wit and imbecile to be tying himself up in matrimony at such a tender age. At twenty-three, he should be making the most of his youth and freedom, they had pointed out. They would be adventuring abroad, soaring their wild wings where their fancy took them, free to do exactly as they pleased, whilst poor Hugh would be forced to trim his wings according to his wife's wishes. Ordinarily, Hugh took his friends' teasing in good humour, laughing and countering their jibes with his own. On that occasion, however unintentionally, they had endorsed his doubts as to the wisdom of so early and hasty a marriage. Those doubts had become more akin to certainties, he reflected, remembering that his wife's attitude had been no different during the last ten days of their honeymoon from at the start.

Unaware of her young husband's feelings, Tracy was in the best of moods. Unaware that Hugh's thoughts were elsewhere, she had engaged in an idle chat and continued quite volubly. With an effort, Hugh tried to match his wife's preoccupation with her social acquaintances.

On their return to Salisbury, she had toured their new house fussing interminably about even a speck of dust. She spent each morning exhorting the maid to clean and polish more assiduously and even to remake the cushions each time they had been flattened, so that at no time ever did a single object in their home look out of place or used.

Tracy was quite unaware how foreign her attitude was to him, Hugh thought, for he had grown up for the most part in the bachelor atmosphere of Umtali where he, his grandfather and father had been content to allow the housekeeper to maintain her own standards. The dogs' hairs upon the carpet, the muddy shoe prints on the polished floors were part of their way of life in the country.

Hugh's thoughts turned inevitably at this point to his grandfather, who was far from well now that his gout had worsened. The old man's heart was upon Hugh's marriage, he had taken the journey to Salisbury for the wedding, and despite his obvious fatigue, he had been clearly happy and delighted to see his grandson married. In fact, Hugh thought now, had it not been for his grandfather's obsessive wish to see him married, he would not have thought of settling down than his friends, especially with a woman he hardly knew.

Yet the Tracy who now shared his life and home was not so different, he thought uneasily, from the bossy little girl he had disliked in his childhood. He would have to take a firm hand with her in the future. He had probably been too loose during their honeymoon in his attempt to soften her heart a little. Not together, Tracy was altogether unloving. She responded with affectionate kisses and loving smiles when he paid her a compliment or gave her some little present. If she seemed to want to avoid his company at night in the bedroom, she made up for it during the day, requiring him to be constantly by her side.

She was not happy unless he was attending upon her, he thought, his restiveness increasing.

Despite the warmth of the room, he shivered. There seemed to have been a chill around his heart ever since he had returned to Salisbury. His home no longer seemed the same familiar establishment, and he did not feel at ease in it.

Tracy had had it redecorated and refurbished during the month preceding their wedding, and although he approved of much of the beautiful new furniture she had selected, he missed the familiar antiques that long ago, his mother had chosen for the house. The plain fact was that he was always pleased to be out of the place.

With an impulsiveness that was typical of him, he suddenly stood up and said in a firm voice that left no room for argument. 'I am going out with my friends after all, Tracy, so do not wait up for me. I am really not of any use to you here.'

The astonished expression on her face revealed her shock and dismay. 'But Hugh, sweetie...'

Her protest died on her lips as she saw the flash of anger in his eyes, the first time he had ever shown this emotion. Quickly, she altered her tone as she rose from the chair to go to him. 'Of course you are longing to see your friends after so long,' she said tenderly. 'That is being selfish of me, wanting to keep you at my side. But do not be too long away, my darling, as I shall miss you sorely!'

Her murmur was softly seductive and for a moment, Hugh hesitated. *Was it possible that suddenly, when he had given up all hope, that Tracy had a change of heart or at least a surge of emotion?* If he were to return early, would Tracy be waiting for him in the bedroom with a look of welcome on her face?

His eyes travelled swiftly over her figure. It was not voluptuous, and the swell of her breasts, which he had observed before their marriage, had been assisted by padding, he now knew. Her skin was young and smooth and fresh, silky to his touch, and despite everything, he was not without desire for her.

She was brushing her lips against his cheek the first approach she had ever made of her own accord. As Hugh put his hand beneath her chin and turned her face so that he could kiss her lips, he discovered them cold and firmly closed against his tongue.

With a sigh, he drew back from her and said lightly, 'Do not wait up for me, my dear. I will see you at breakfast.'

Hugh was meeting with three of his closest friends. They greeted him warmly. 'We have missed you, old fellow.'

'How is marriage life, eh?'

'Let us drive down to Salisbury?' another suggested.

'Oliver Mutukudzi has a gig and I have heard that many beautiful ladies often amuse themselves there.'

'We can't have Hugh blotting his marriage certificate soon after his marriage!' Quipped another. 'He can enjoy the music and we will enjoy the girls!'

Once again Hugh's spirits fell, but only momentarily. He was not going to allow his marriage to change his life all that much. And after the disaster of his honeymoon with Tracy, he would enjoy a romp with any female who really appreciated what he had to offer.

In the end, Hugh's faithfulness to Tracy was not put to test. The road they were to take was under construction and it was in turn jammed by heavy traffic. They ended up going at a local bar for their rounds of beer listening to Oliver Mtukudzi's music. After the outrageous night, men were found to drive Hugh and his friends to their homes, not one of them being in a state to drive himself.

Tracy woke from a light sleep to the sound of Hugh's raised voice and that of the maid trying to quieten him. She sat upright, her head on one side, listening. There was no doubt that her young husband was drunk, she thought furiously. At least this would be one night when she had every possible excuse to refuse his presence in her bed. Not that he had given her reason to suppose he might come to her room when he returned from the club. On the contrary, he had expressly told her not to wait up for him. Nevertheless, she would have to upbraid him in the morning, gently and sweetly, of course, so that he did not begin to think of her as a tyrant.

'It is the only way to achieve what you want my dear,' her mother had said during those last few weeks prior to her wedding, when she had thought Tracy should be warned of the less obvious facets of married life. 'You do not want to give him grounds for taking a mistress...'

According to her mother, a mistress was an almost unavoidable evil if a wife refused her husband his marital rights. Although the good lady did not actually say so in many words, Tracy gathered that her mother had done just this and thrown her father into the arms of a more willing female. Of course, there was nothing a wife could do if such a thing happened, other than pretend to her women friends, who would certainly gossip about it, either that she did not know or she did not care.

A mistress was to be avoided at all costs, since it was not unknown for a husband to end up preferring such a woman's company to that of his wife, who could then risk the terrible consequence of being turned out of her own home to make room for her rival. 'It is really quite unfair,' her mother had admitted to the round-eyed Tracy. 'But such is life, my dear. You must never forget that a man is the superior of a woman, born with more intelligence and a greater understanding of life. God has created them so, and those strange women one hears about of late who profess themselves the equal of men are to be abhorred.'

Moreover her mother had added, they courted disaster for themselves, since were they to pursue their beliefs, they would very soon find themselves at serious loggerheads not only with society, but with their husbands.

When at last Tracy dozed off to sleep again, it was without resolving the conflict of opinions that had disturbed her equilibrium. She had yet to make up her mind how she would *manage* Hugh, since *managing* him was the most important thing in her life now that at long last she was his wife.

There had not been one morning since her wedding when she had not woken to a feeling of intense satisfaction that he was hers at last. Not one of her friends had a husband as devastatingly attractive, as charming, amusing or as popular as Hugh.

She genuinely loved him. His four sisters declared that he was *wild* and *irresponsible*, that he liked women, hunting them, flirting with them, even seducing them, and causing his family not a little concern lest he should involve them all in some dreadful scandal, young though he was. There had never been anyone else Tracy wished to marry and she had been steadfast in her determination to wait for him.

When Tracy woke up the next morning, she was no longer in doubt about it. Gently, persuasively, so that he barely noticed it, Hugh must be broken-in like an unruly young male horse and made to toe her line.

The following day was much worse than the previous one, if that was possible. The sad news had really sunk in, their father was indeed dead. Gone. Heartbroken and pained as they were, they still had to make the necessary arrangements for the funeral.

The funeral parlour and church had to be called. Friends and relatives had to be notified as well. This was a very demanding and emotionally draining procedure because their father had been a very socially active and well-known man.

They couldn't trust their mother with anything. The old woman was still dumbstruck and too pained to do anything useful. They all were, but somebody had to be strong and deal with the nasty affairs. Since they didn't have a male sibling, it meant that it was their duty to make the arrangements.

As the day progressed, many long forgotten relatives dropped by wailing dramatically in exaggerated pain whilst flailing onto the cold hard ground.

Their father's workmates, in designer suits also passed by offering their heartfelt condolences. They also insisted on financial assistance for the funeral even though it wasn't needed.

The sisters' friends also came for moral support. All this didn't help lighten the mood. As each new person came, a new tidal wave of pain and weeping floated in the atmosphere. They also had to explain what had transpired to everyone who came or called.

By nightfall, they were exhausted. Not by mere handling of the funeral's logistics, but by other kind of brawls.

It was annoying how easily the funeral was turned to focus on other insignificant things other than the deceased. People had ended the day fighting for stolen meat.

'This cheapens the memory of a great man. I mean, how could Tete Vaida fuss over stolen meat at her brother's funeral?' Rochelle fumed.

That night, Rutendo asked Rochelle to slow down. 'You cannot solve everything Rochelle please slow down or we might end up losing you too. Fatigue and stress can be consuming little devils.'

Rochelle smiled weakly at her little sister and confided the truth to her. 'I already feel like everyone's Mom, including our mother,' she said gesturing to their mother who was gazing blankly at the ceiling murmuring incoherently. She was far too gone.

ZIMBABWE
HARARE, 1980

Hugh's phone rang and for a confused moment, he thought it was somebody else calling, for a lot was on his mind.

'Darling, where are you?'

As always, Tracy began with those words. He never asked her where she was when he called her, but she would tell him anyway. It was as if she needed the reassurance of their physicality when they were not together. She had a high girlish voice. They were supposed to be at her friend's house for the party at seven thirty pm. It was already past six. He told her he was in traffic.

'But it's moving. I'm coming.'

As the gateman opened the gate, Hugh looked at his house. Inside was his furniture imported from overseas, his wife, his sister and their maid, Rudo. The rooms would all be cool, air conditioner vents swaying quietly and the kitchen would be fragrant with curry. The TV set would be turned to BBC.

He climbed out of the car. In the past months, he had begun, to feel bloated from all he had acquired. He was not sure, he had in fact never been sure, whether he liked his wealth or he liked it because he was supposed to.

'Darling,' Tracy said, opening the door before he got to it. She was all made up, her complexion glowing. He thought, as he often did, what a beautiful woman she was. She had a startling symmetry to her features. Her silk dress made her figure look very *hourglassy*.

He hugged her carefully avoiding her lips, painted pink and lined in a darker pink. 'You look pretty,' he said

She laughed. The same way she laughed, with an open, accepting enjoyment of her own looks when people complimented her looks.

'Will you bath or just change?' Tracy asked following him upstairs where she had laid up a blue slim fit suit on the bed. He would have preferred a simple shirt and a pair of jeans. He didn't like this outfit with its overly decorative embroidery, which Tracy had bought for an outrageous sum from one of those new pretentious designer shops abroad. He would wear it to please her.

'I will just change,' he said.

'How was work?' She asked in the vague, pleasant way she always asked.

As soon as they arrived at the party, Tracy led the way around the room, hugging men and women she barely knew. She called the older ones *Ma* and *Sir* with exaggerated respect, basking in the attention her face drew. She flattened her personality so that her beauty did not threaten. She praised a woman's dress, a man's tie. She said, 'We thank God,' often. When a woman asked her in an accusing tone, 'What cream do you use on your face? How can one person have this kind of perfect skin?' Tracy laughed graciously and promised to send the woman a letter with details of her skin care routine.

Hugh had always been struck by how important it was to her to be a wholesomely agreeable person, to have no sharp angles sticking out.

On Sunday, she would invite his relatives for lunch and then made sure everyone was suitably overfed. She ended every sentence she addressed to his uncle with *sir*. There was something immodest about her modesty. It announced itself.

ZIMBABWE, HARARE
CHISHAWASHA HILLS, 2016

The funeral itself had been successful. One by one, the relatives left for their homes leaving the deceased's family alone. Days passed and they were trying to heal save for their mother who was slipping bit by bit from them. She had lost weight drastically and was terribly thin. She had dark shadows underneath her eyes and seemed always on the verge of tears. She jumped at the slightest noise and also became increasingly irate. She had nightmares and no longer attended church. Their mother no longer had a life and they feared for her. They feared for her sanity.

Because of all this, Rochelle had decided that they should take turns to stay with their mother until she had taken full control of her life. They ignored their mother's weak refusal to this. 'You girls shouldn't give up your independent lives for me. I'm a responsible adult and I. I don't need a babysitter,' she said.

The sisters always made sure to accommodate her in their activities. They also began trusting her with minor responsibilities so that she could keep her mind off things.

Rutendo later complained about mother's complacence to Rochelle.

'This is not fair at all. We have all lost a person whom we loved deeply. I can't deny that it has been a huge blow in the gut, but Mom makes it seem like she is the only one who was hurt. I feel like I have grown a few decades older in the past week.'

Rochelle kept quiet for a moment thinking of the best way to respond to her sister, but before she could respond, Rutendo continued.

'Face it, Rochelle, Mom has turned into a baby. A very huge cry baby.'

'Please don't say that. You know very well that it is a different story for us than Mom. Dad was her soul mate. These guys have lived together for more than half their lives together. She was dependent in every way possible on Dad. So I think saying what you just said is being selfish and rude,' Rochelle admonished her younger sister.

'I understand, Rochelle, but I think that Mom is taking away our childhood.'

Rochelle let out a wry laugh and then she shook her head sideways as she spoke. 'Childhood? How funny. You are a mother, but here you are saying Mom is taking away your childhood.'

Unknowingly, Rutendo had awakened Rochelle's fears. She became increasingly aware that she was now thirty-seven and childless.

ZIMBABWE, HARARE
CHISHAWASHA HILLS, 2016

The reading of the will had been the last painful reminder of their deceased father.

When the day arrived the solemnity and glum of the receding weeks returned. The residents of the house became increasingly aware of their loved one's death.

The lawyer, a very short heavy set and balding old man, arrived around eleven in the morning. He just had that look of a corrupt politician. A glutton. The way he was looking at Natsai, who was openly flirting with him, made Rochelle almost throw up in revolt. The man had to be at least a decade older than their father.

After a few minutes, they had all settled in the spacious sitting room.

'Apart from a few minor bequests,' the lawyer said coolly, 'Your father has left everything to his children.'

A learned lawyer herself, Rochelle didn't miss the use of the phrase, *his children*.

'Hold on. What do you mean by, his children? It would seem for a tiny moment that there are other children aside from us in this room,' she said hotly glowering.

'How clever. You must be Rochelle. Your father told me a lot about you. I'm impressed,' he said peering at Rochelle above his tiny spectacles slightly amused by Rochelle's outburst. 'It would be wise if I read your father's exact words from the will.'

Their mother, heartbroken shuttered poor mother looked like she would faint and shifted uncomfortably on the couch. Rochelle, who was sitting next to their mother, instinctively held her in an embrace. She had become a mother hen in the past few weeks.

'In case of my death, apart from a few minor bequests clarified under Clause 2.2.1, I leave some of the Estate and money to my four daughters,' at this news there was a collective gasp of shock from the sisters, 'Rochelle, Rutendo, Natsai and Rose in...'

The old man went on reading, but he had lost his audience, the sisters were no longer paying any attention. The blow had hit home. Natsai looked the worst, hyperventilating and beads of perspiration on her pretty face ruining the expensive rouge she had applied. Rutendo looked ashen and Rochelle, the ever-calm Rochelle, was shaking. It was their mother who surprised them all. She didn't look a bit taken aback nor was she angry. Instead, she wore a guilty expression. It was evident that she knew something they didn't.

'Preposterous!' Rochelle shouted, 'Mom please speak up, how can Dad have four daughters without us knowing?' She implored, but nobody missed the edge to her voice. It was a diplomatic demand for explanation from their mother.

'This is a lie mother, isn't it? Please tell us that it is just a big confusion or joke or maybe this bastard is lying,' pleaded Rutendo.

Their mother sighed. When she spoke, her voice was choked with emotion. 'I never intended for you to find out this way. I never wanted you to tarnish that beautiful memory you had of your father.' Tears fell freely from their mother's well-plastered gaunt cheeks.

'But, Mom if he had the guts to go and screw around the union then I'm afraid he isn't worth honouring. That man is a fraud.' Coming from Natsai, that was a surprise. She was the quietest although the most mischievous and closest to their parents.

'Young lady, don't you dare say that! He is still your father,' her mother said sternly.

'Yes, Mom, I can't deny that, but I never thought he would be capable of doing that.'

'We all make mistakes,' their mother said 'What matters is that I forgave him.'

The slow speaking, but quick thinking Rochelle spoke up at last with a hoarse voice full of emotion. 'Mother, I think you are being unfair. Let us deal with the shocking news in our own way. It's still fresh to us, you on the other hand has had time to heal. You have known it for a long time.'

'That's true Mom. You can't expect to throw such news in our faces and expect us to stay calm,' Rutendo said slowly nodding to what her sister had just said.

'So tell us mother, who is this half-sister of ours? We have to know her,' said Natsai with a surprising touch of coolness to her voice.

'Yes, mother tell us,' Rochelle said trying to act civilised and calm.

It was obviously difficult for their mother to open up. Although she had been putting up a show in defending her dead husband a few minutes ago, she now seemed vulnerable and openly in pain.

'Her name is Rosein,' her voice was distant. 'Rosein Dube.'

ZIMBABWE
HARARE, 1981

Wearing a pair of black slacks, high heeled stilettos and very expensive jewellery, Tracy got out of her car. She took of her tinted shades revealing her flawless expensive makeup on a perfect face with well-toned silky skin. Her hair, black to the root, fell perfectly to her shoulders leaving her long graceful neck in open view. Her skin had a natural glow and she was radiating, she was a beauty. With her purse in hand, she walked in through the main entrance of the Truman and Truman Law Firm. She walked past the reception into the elevator, ignoring the greetings from Gloria her receptionist. As she got in the second floor, people were just murmuring their greetings to her and yet like a stone, she couldn't be bothered. That was Tracy Truman's usual self. She couldn't be bothered. She opened the door to her office, which was at the far end of the corridor and it had the engraving, *Managing Partner T. Truman*. It was exactly 7.30 A.M.

'Morning, Madam,' this was Nyasha her secretary.

'How many times do I have to tell you it's Ma'am, not Madam?' Quipped Tracy.

'Sorry, Ma'am. Your coffee will be in your office in a minute.' This was a result of routine. Everything was planned in advance.

'Here, your coffee, just as you like it,' Nyasha said as she got into the adjoining room which was Tracy's office.

'Any news?' Asked Tracy. This was so typical of her. Not even a sign of gratitude for the coffee.

'No, Ma'am.'

'Did you deliver the paperwork as I instructed you to?'

'Yes,' Nyasha answered.

'It's *"Yes, Ma'am,"'* chimed in Tracy. Just like every other day, conversations were kept short and brusque. 'One more thing Nyasha,' Tracy said as she removed her blazer. 'No disturbances today. I'm busy.'

'Yes, Ma'am,' Nyasha then closed the door behind her and got into her office. She then stood behind the closed door and let a huge sigh of relief. She then opened the top button of her shirt, it was hot. She grimaced when she thought of what Tracy's reaction would be like if she saw her dressed in this manner. She had made it clear from the very first day she had noticed Nyasha with an open top button that she detested it. She considered such behaviour to be unprofessional and to be expected only from inexperienced staff. It was petty things most workers overlooked such as this that led to the loss of dignified clients, she had been told. She moved and took a seat by her desk, raised her head. 'It's yes Ma'am,' she mimicked Tracy.

Tracy's office was well furnished with top class decorum. With a huge desk with neatly piled papers, a porcelain vase with fresh water dahlias and a new typewriter. There were highly polished marble tiles in the room. She opened the French door leading to the balcony. Her coffee mug in hand. On the wall was a huge picture frame, which had a picture of her and her husband, Hugh, who was also her business partner. She drew a deep breath. Every morning, Tracy liked to just relax before really getting lost in her work. With her back to the noisy street, she seemed to inspect her office and smiled. Her achievements always made her happy and satisfied. She was surely living her dream. A result of hard work. She was really enjoying the fresh morning air alongside her coffee.

It was then that the phone rang.

She scurried to her desk to answer. It was Nyasha. 'Ma'am, there is a man here who wants to see you.'

'What did I tell you? Tell him I'm busy.'

'He says it's urgent.'

'What's his name?' Tracy had a deep frown giving her an ugly depression on her forehead.

'He won't say. He says it will ruin the surprise.'

There was a short pause, in which Tracy was thinking of how to respond. A deep furrow on her forehead.

She let out a sigh and murmured something to herself about people who never knew the importance of appointments before proceeding. 'Let him in.'

Within a few seconds, the door was opened. He walked in. Tracy felt a pang in her stomach when she saw whom it was. Her jaw involuntarily dropped, but she could not bring herself to utter a single word.

Was she hallucinating again? He had changed a lot. The once muscular and well-toned body was now nothing more than a skeleton. The usual healthy glowing dark skin was now almost coal black. It also seemed like he was recovering from facial herpes. He must have obviously noticed her unmasked shock because he said, 'Well that's what you get after staying your whole life in the countryside without proper medication and food,' he said forcing a smile on his mouth.

'Tafara?' That's all Tracy could say.

'Still proud of my native name and of being African too,' he said fixing his gaze on her face. He had stopped and was standing at the centre of the big room. Tracy indicated for him to take a seat, which he took willingly. 'They tell me I'm wasting away. The cancer came back with much power this time. It's only a matter of months,' he continued. 'Devastating isn't it? Too bad, I can't afford proper medication. Truth be told, I can hardly afford to feed twice a day or lead an expensive life like you, Tracy.'

She winced.

'I want you to come home with me, Darling. To our home, to family, to our son. Sweetheart come home to me,' Tafara said this moving on to the French door behind Tracy's desk. He put his hands in the pockets of his trousers and waited a while. 'Does he know that you have a son? Does he know you aborted our unborn child because you wanted to go to university? Does he know that's the reason why you can't conceive right now? I bet he will be very happy to hear this from me,' Tafara said as he took a seat on Tracy's desk.

As soon as he sat, Tracy stood up and began pacing for a while. She then stood still and said in a quiet voice. 'So is this why you are here? To blackmail me? Trust me, it won't work.'

'You are scared as hell, I can tell. Remember I can read you like an open book. So please stop pretending,' Tafara shot back. Tracy ran her hands in her hair and smiled. 'You are pathetic dear, it won't work. What makes you so sure that Hugh will listen to you? Look at you.'

It is not like she is lying, reasoned Tafara in her mind. *This won't work.*

He took a deep breath and moved from the desk on which he was sitting and stood looking into the big picture frame on the wall. He smiled. 'You married a white man after all.'

Tracy smiled back. 'His name is Hugh and we own this place. We also have a lovely adorable baby girl named Rochelle,' she said.

'To actually think that when I first heard that you changed your name I couldn't believe it. I thought people were just jealous, you know how it is back home. But then I come here and I call you Tracy and you seem to enjoy it. Are you now ashamed of your native name, Rumbidzai? The once proud Zimbabwean lady I knew, I'm ashamed of you.'

'Please stop your vile attacks, Tafara. Everyone has a right to live freely, even if they choose to change their names. It is important to note that you could have never managed to give me a life I always yearned for,' she said sounding all together uninterested in the conversation. 'I mean, you can't afford this kind of life I know I deserve,' she said pacing around the office.

'So this is what it is about? It's all about the

money? Not love?' Tafara replied hardly covering his surprise.

'Yes, to some extent. Don't be naive. I won't take you back in my life, Tafara and I'm not sorry, I have moved on and so should you.'

'I can see you have grown tougher, not the shy girl I used to know.'

She let a laugh escape through her clenched teeth. 'Yes. You have to be tough to achieve an empire like this. I'm busy, Tafara. It's now time for me to work. You have to leave,' she said matter-of-factly.

He could hardly believe that this lady had once loved him neither could he believe that he had once made love to her. A woman he had first knew in bed, herself a virgin. They had a child together. Now this woman, whom his heart sorely ached for was telling him to leave without showing any kind of emotion or remorse. How he had, in his young years, imagined a perfect small happy family with this lady. Reality held a torture to his being. A constant reminder that once you bring someone close to your heart and show them your flaws, you should be prepared to be hurt. These people who claim to love you when they leave your life, it's like a whirlwind or rather, being hit by a wrecking ball. They destroy your trust, your confidence, bruising your ego along the way. Such a detrimental effect. Total emasculation.

He was disturbed from his thoughts by Tracy's voice. 'Will you please excuse me, Mr Chara? I need to get busy.'

Tafara was perturbed. She had never called him by his surname before. 'How can your love be fickle and selective Rumbidzai? Have you already forgotten all I did for you? Tell me, how could you look at me and not see all I have done for you?'

'Don't be so crass, Tafara. We get to grow and realise our mistakes. Now if you could excuse me now, before I call security, I would appreciate it,' she had raised her voice by now all her grace and innocence lost. 'I need some fresh air,' she said leaving for the balcony.

ZIMBABWE, HARARE
CHISHAWASHA HILLS, 2016

'Rosein Dube!' Bellowed Rutendo. They had all been thrown off balance.

'You can't possibly be referring to, Rosein, the slut!' Put in Rochelle hotly.

'Rochelle, you don't have to call your sister a slut,' her mother highlighted weakly.

Rosein and Rochelle, although years apart, were rivals. It had all started when the former snatched the latter's boyfriend.

Because of this *treasonous* act alone, Rochelle had grown a strong hatred for Rosein. To Rochelle, it felt almost like a miracle that Rosein still frequented their home since she, Rochelle, would always radiate waves of hatred. Rosein was Natsai's best friend.

That night when they had retired to bed, Rochelle and Rutendo sneaked into their baby sister's room. This was a childhood habit. The room was the furthest from their parents' bedroom. This meant that they could hold a decent conversation in the deep hours of the day without being overheard by their parents. They joked around a few minor issues, but they knew that coiled deep in each one of them was the need to discuss the day's proceedings. They gradually unravelled the issue.

'The funny part is that Rosein is a year older than Natsai. I just don't get it,' Rutendo said filing her nails.

Rochelle sighed and took a generous swig of tea from her mug. 'To think that all this time our parents had been keeping this from us, it's just enraging. Dad knew that I called her a slut. How unoriginal,' she let out a dry laugh.

'Forgive me people, but I'm starting to think that our father was a hypocrite,' Rutendo said slowly.

They smiled weakly at each other.

'Natsai, how do you take it? I mean, Rosein has been your best friend in like forever,' Rochelle asked with keen interest.

'I know I'm not supposed to enjoy this or anything, but I think it's kind of cool. We won't be just like sisters anymore, we would be sisters,' she smiled sheepishly.

Her older sisters looked at each other in exasperated disdain. They reproved of this.

'How can you be this shallow, Natsai?' Rutendo asked.

'Daddy messed up, I can't deny that, but it's just like Mom said, we should forgive him and move on with our lives.'

As she was saying this, Rochelle and Rutendo looked at as if she had gone mad. It was ludicrous that their sister could be so shallow and narrow-minded. They had expected more from her. The more independent and carefree of all the sisters. She was supposed to be the fire. She had let them down.

'Natsai, dear, we are talking about what Dad did. He cheated on Mom and you are just okay with that? How can you be this calm?' Rochelle said, almost pleading.

'Darling, I think that Rochelle is right. How can you just be fine with that?' Rutendo chimed in.

'That is your problem guys. Even when we were young, it was only your opinion to things that mattered. My view to things doesn't matter at all. I'm young and I'm neither a doctor nor a lawyer like you guys, but I'm not thick,' Natsai tried to feign indifference, but you couldn't miss a slight edge in her sugary voice.

Her older siblings just looked at each other with mere surprise. This was the first time Natsai had ever spoken up to any of them. She was beginning to find herself.

They would soon discover that many things had changed pertaining to Rachael. She was no longer a sweet and innocent girl.

ZIMBABWE
HARARE, 1988

'I am extremely sorry, Mr Truman. We did everything we possibly could to save the baby. I am afraid Tracy had an unusually prolonged labour. When the baby finally came into the world, it was too late. Your wife however should make a good recovery in due course.'

Hugh looked away from the sympathetic gaze of the gynaecologist who had attended the birth. The doctor had an excellent reputation, and Hugh assumed that if he had been unable to save the baby, no one else could have done so.

In his life, he had never been as unhappy, or more devastated. Bitterly, he reflected that had the stillborn lived, it would have obviated the necessity for Tracy to have more children. He had wanted a son. One son would have been sufficient, provided he was strong and healthy.

Hugh paused outside the door. In common decency, he must try to hide his disappointment and lessen Tracy's, he told himself. Judging by the commotion of the last twenty-four hours, she had suffered a great deal and it was not even as if she wanted the baby in the first place. She had hidden the signs as long as she decently could, wearing flowing, concealing dresses until she was within two months of the birth. She had made Hugh promise on his oath not to tell anyone until the secret could no longer be kept.

Was it possible that her insistence on carrying out all her normal occupations had contributed to this difficult and fatal birth? He asked himself. He owed it to her to try now to be sympathetic, kindly and loving. *It will not be easy.* He did not love her, and that was the whole unfortunate truth. After five years of marriage, they were still very little in common, and daily, the bonds of marriage became more irksome to him.

With a feeling close to despair, Hugh went into their room. She was lying in the vast double bed, propped up by a small mountain of pillows. Her hair was tied back from her exhausted face with a blue ribbon matching those on her nightgown. Her eyes were closed. Their maid sitting in a chair beside the bed vacated it immediately when she saw Hugh. She put a finger to her lips.

'Madam is sleeping!' She mouthed.

With a sense of relief, which was hard, to conceal, backed out of the room. He really did not feel up to consoling Tracy at the moment, when he himself felt so inconsolable. If indeed she required comforting, he told himself bitterly, as he went back to the empty lounge.

Maybe Tracy's reluctance to share her bed with him was in part due to her wish to avoid the resultant pregnancies. Tracy must have known they were unavoidable when she agreed to marry him. Naturally, they had not discussed so intimate a subject before marriage. It was only afterwards that he had learned of her attitude to motherhood.

They had to have a child despite Tracy's views. Children were key to success in marriage. He believed that marriages could not hold ground without these fruits to show. These were considered as gifts from the above. He knew that by now everyone was beginning to talk and speculate.

He poured himself another drink and sat down in the high winged chair, stretching out his long legs as he became aware of his tiredness. He had had very little sleep the previous night. The issue was consuming him and he began to fear for his sanity. Perhaps his present fatigue was in part responsible for his depression, he told himself. *Was it the big empty room?* His home was more like a museum, everything perfectly in place, beautiful, but soulless and he felt like a prisoner in it – always anxious, as he was now, to escape.

ZIMBABWE, HARARE
CHISHAWASHA HILLS, 2016

The environment at number 12 Chishawasha Hills place turned alarmingly gloomier with the arrival of Rosein. The ever-exuberant Rutendo became more quiet than usual, and visited less using her spending more time at home with her kids as an excuse. Rochelle spent more hours outside than inside the house, working late hours and extra shifts for a *good cause*. When they, Rochelle and Rutendo, were home, which was seldom, they locked themselves in their rooms hours on end.

If it was possible, their mother had grown even thinner and shaky. Rochelle had secretly confided in Rutendo that they ought to find her professional help. Natsai was the only one who seemed unaffected by the transition at all. She was too happy to have Rosein as her sister to notice the weird display of hatred by her sisters.

Poor Rosein seemed torn among the ever-moody bigger sisters, happy young sister and wary stepmother.

One fateful day, Rochelle and Rutendo weren't going to work and all hell broke loose. Rochelle had been walking around the house a bit flustered about something. Rosein in her overly sweet nature had wished the former a very good morning.

'You know what? My morning would be a lot better if you just leave now,' sharply retorted Rochelle.

Caught unaware, Rosein didn't know how to respond. Unfortunately, Rochelle felt like being trouble, she couldn't just let the opportunity pass by. 'I just don't get it Rosein. What more do you intend to get by staying here? What do you want from my family Rosein?'

'Rochelle, this is my family too and you are my sister. I am here because we are sisters and we have to stick together now more than ever.' Rosein replied coolly.

'Yeah, right, that's working wonderfully don't you agree?' She made sure that Rosein would get the sarcasm.

'I still think it's worth a try don't you think?' Rosein wouldn't be put off.

'Maybe you have overstayed your welcome. Or just maybe you were never welcome in the first place,' Rochelle's words hit a wall.

Rosein didn't reply. She had no option, but to add sweetly while staring into Rosein's eyes all the while. 'You know I hate you, right?'

Her stepsister merely smirked, stood up with a crooked smile on her lips, 'Don't worry big sister. The feeling has always been mutual.'

ZIMBABWE, HARARE
CROWNE PLAZZA HOTEL, 2016

At a hotel nearby Chishawasha Hills, two lovers lay naked in bed in each other's arms. The atmosphere was dripping of sex and stale semen's odour clung in the air. Both were sex satiated and reeking of sweat. Neither was speaking. They lay quiet, the girl's head on the guy's chest.

It was the girl, a very attractive young lady in her twenties who broke the silence. 'I have to get ready and go.'

'You know I hate this,' Whispered the man in a husky voice. 'I wish you could stay.'

'Oh don't be silly, Trevor. I'm sure your wife must be missing you,' she said playfully.

He avoided the statement. 'You know that I love you very much.'

It was a statement, but she answered all the same. 'Yes, I do. No doubt about that,' she said as she got up from the queen-sized bed. She was naked. She started arranging her hair in front of the mirror.

'What would you say if I said let's elope? You know I would do that for you right?'

Trevor finished saying this standing a breath behind the young lady. He was so close that she could feel his breathe hot at her neck. She stopped laughing and turned.

'Trevor, No! I can't. You are a married man for God's sake.'

'That means nothing. I'm a married man, but here

we are. We just got out of bed,' he smiled coyly.

She couldn't help, but smile, a little. He was like that at times. Reckless. 'You know what? Your wife really loves you. You should see the way she parades you. I almost feel guilty. The key word being, almost,' she smiled and stole a quick kiss on his mouth.

'So what do you say sexy?' Trevor kept on insisting. He could be as stubborn as a mule at times.

'You sure aren't going to give up on this are you?'

'No, I am not,' he said firmly.

She sighed in exasperation. 'Trevor, I can't do this. You know I can't. I don't have to punish her that way. She is my sister for crying out loud.'

'It's like I said, Natsai, you are still sleeping with your sister's husband.'

They argued for a long time to no avail.

Trevor admired Natsai. He had always done, ever since that fateful day two years back when they had first had sex. It had been an avoidable devil. Both enjoying the sex in diabolical gusto. She had been unhappy and vulnerable and he had been there to comfort her. They had both had sex as pay back to Rochelle's controlling ways. That entire nagging and motherly role she held wherever they went. They both were victims.

The double life had started induced by this mutual feeling. Thus he cheated on Rochelle, his wife, her sister.

After they had argued about whether to elope or not, Natsai and Trevor were to be seen stripping naked again both in for another round of steamy hot sex.

They both didn't get to their respective homes that night.

At that very moment, when they had had just reached climaxes, Rochelle was home worried sick about Natsai. She had never slept outside the house without notifying her.

Rochelle, the mother hen.

ZIMBABWE
VICTORIA FALLS, 1988

The room was in semi-darkness. A white aproned nurse sat at one side of the bed. The private doctor stood at the other side, his hand around Hugh's dying grandfather's wrist. He shook his head and moved away to make room for Hugh.

There was a lump at Hugh's throat as he gazed down at the frail, white haired old man lying propped against the pillows. Swallowing hard, he bent over. 'It is Hugh, grandfather.'

Slowly with an obvious effort, the dying man's eyelids lifted, and his eyes focused on his grandson. A faint smile lifted the corners of his mouth. His breathing was very shallow and seemed to Hugh to be intermittent. He realized how very deeply he loved this old man. He longed to cry aloud.

'Do not die, grandfather. You must not die. I need you...'

There was a question in this old fellow's eyes, which without a spoken word, Hugh understood. 'Yes it is good news, just what you are waiting to hear, grandfather. Tracy gave birth to a son yesterday evening, a fine boy weighing three kilograms. I now have an heir to continue the Truman dynasty. I came straightaway to tell you...' His voice faltered and stopped as he saw his grandfather's eyes close. The face was peaceful as he drew a long shuddering breath and then was still.

Hugh, his face strained, stopped to kiss the gaunt

cheek. Then, without a word, he walked out of the room.

The last words I ever spoke to him were lies, he thought despairingly. There seemed to be no alternative for all he wanted was for him to be happy. Tormented by his thoughts, his feet took him automatically into the study, the room where his grandfather had spent so many of his last months of life. He walked slowly around the big room, drawing back the heavy curtains. These few days had been too much for him. Though he was a man, it was too much to bear. He sorely loved his grandfather. He had been more of a father figure to him in all his life.

There was a discreet knock on the door and the maid came into the room to say that the family lawyer Mr Rwafa, had come and wished to speak with him. 'Ask him what it is about,' Hugh said, frowning. 'I really do not wish to be bothered for the moment.'

The maid departed only to return a moment later with a note from Rwafa stating that there were certain matters regarding the birth of his son which he required discussion in so far as they affected his grandfather's will. 'Show him in,' he instructed the maid, suddenly aware that any company at this moment of depression was better than his own.

It was the first time that Hugh had met Rwafa. He eyed the small, sharp featured young man with much the same instinctive aversion, as had his grandfather before him. He listened impatiently while the lawyer offered his condolences, and then in a sharper tone than he had intended, Hugh said, 'Your business must be urgent, Rwafa, since you felt it necessary to see me this early and my grandfather's body not yet cold.'

Rwafa nodded, his emotions too well controlled to betray his irritation at the implied rebuke. He resented Hugh's proud, haughty tone, and he resented the expensive clothes he was wearing. 'Your grandfather, apart from a few minor bequests, has left everything to you. There are however two houses set up, one for your brother Takudzwa, and another for the eldest son born to you. The Doctor has told me that Tracy has just presented you with a fine healthy boy, so the house...'

Biting his lower lip, Hugh broke in harshly. 'You have been misinformed, sir. My wife gave birth to a male infant yesterday, but it was a stillborn. I omitted this fact when I informed my grandfather, since I wished to make his last moments here on earth happy ones. So since, you seem to consider this house important at such a time, it is best you know the facts, all the facts. My wife and I will have no further children.'

Rwafa suppressed his surprise at this bland statement. Beneath Hugh's harsh tone was bitterness and pain. 'My most sincere apologies to you Hugh,' he murmured. He looked at Hugh and added tentatively. 'There is perhaps an option. Your grandfather took certain actions to safeguard you from... shall we say an unfortunate little incident in your life that could have resulted in your undoing...'

Slowly, relentlessly, he unfolded the previous year's summer and its consequences. There was disbelief when he first heard it. Gradually, Rwafa noted, there dawned an acceptance of the possibility of his culpability. He had, in his drunken, stupor, seduced his grandfather's garden boy's daughter. As soon as her grandfather had noticed that Vimbai was pregnant, he had sent them away on a condition that he would pay their family every month. He had blackmailed the family threatening to expose his father's gay affair. It had struck him as completely unethical. Of course, his grandfather thought he was acting in everyone's best interests. Rwafa said he felt he was obliged to speak since Hugh had a right to know. Yes! He was right. He had had a great timing because it was now he desired a boy child the most.

Hugh ceased his pacing and sat down heavily in one of the armchairs. His thoughts were racing as he tried to think clearly. He still had a hazy recollection of the incident. It followed that a child might have been the result. He bit hard on his lip. None knew how deeply his grandfather had been concerned of the future, especially Hugh's. It was on him all his grandfather's hopes had centred. But right or wrong, the truth remained, he, Hugh had a son, a living son. He knew neither the boy's name nor where he was.

'But why did my grandfather not tell me all this at the time?' He asked Rwafa. 'Surely I, of all people, should have been informed or consulted.'

'Your grandfather was afraid you would feel honourably obliged to marry the girl yourself.'

There was a bitter twist to the corners of Hugh's mouth as he nodded. Of all the suitable candidates he would have married, Tracy had turned out to be the least suitable, or so it seemed. Her social and domestic attributes might be faultless, but as a companion... as a mother...

'Thank you, Rwafa,' Hugh said after a long break. 'Can you then arrange for the baby to be brought to Harare? It too has to be buried, and I would prefer that it lay in the family vault. I am sure you can find a way round any difficulties that may arise.'

'You may leave the matter in my hands,' Rwafa said reassuringly.

Hugh sighed. 'You can't know what a load you have taken off my mind. Last night, as I drove here, my spirits had never been lower. My child had been stillborn and my grandfather was dying. There seemed so little hope for the future. Now... well, my only regret is that my grandfather is not here for me to discuss this with me. It is at least a comfort to me, I did not lie to him at all, and I do have a son after all! I can only look forward to the day that I set my eyes on him.'

Rwafa concealed his smirk of satisfaction. This meeting had gone far much better than he had expected when he had first arrived looking for Hugh. He had not known then about the stillborn baby. His own quick thinking nature had let him turn the situation to his advantage and he congratulated himself for such a short victory. In less than half an hour, Rwafa had managed to give hope to his client and acquired a considerable degree of hope for his own future.

ZIMBABWE, HARARE
CHISHAWASHA HILLS, 2016

'Trust me, Rutendo, you are not going to utter a single word about this to Rochelle or else...' Natsai said coolly to Rutendo, whose face by now was twisted in revulsion.

'Or else what? Tell me, what could you possibly do? You disgust me! He is married to your sister for God's sake. How could you be this cheap?' Rutendo fumed.

She had just found out about the ongoing relationship between Natsai and Trevor. The mere idea that Natsai could agree to be Trevor's mistress was disturbingly preposterous.

Sisters were supposed to have each other's backs not bedding their in-laws. There was absolutely no excuse for that.

Rutendo had always known that Natsai was openly flirtatious and independent, but she never assumed that she could stoop as low as to court her sister's husband.

'Oh, dearie,' chimed Natsai. 'So says the pure lady of virtue.... Mrs Perfect!' The sentence dripped of sarcasm.

Rutendo laughed throwing her head back revealing her perfectly arranged white teeth as she laughed. Natsai was now a lunatic.

'You know, Rutendo, you are very funny. You say all this forgetting what you did four years ago. I might just let it slip over supper...'

She watched Rutendo's face change from angry to horrified as the truth fully registered.

'No, you wouldn't dare,' Rutendo sputtered. 'That's not fair, Natsai. You know that was a wholly different situation. You can't possibly hold me on that.'

Natsai laughed, a diabolical sort of laugh. 'Calm down big sister. You should learn to play nice. The circumstances might have been different, but the harm is now irreversible. Our poor Rochelle wouldn't take that lightly now, would she?'

She shrugged her shoulders as she adjusted herself on the settee. They were all still living at their parents' house. They had all agreed that they would spend the whole year at the old lady's place as she tried to acclimatize to a husband free environment which now seemed like an almost impossible task.

'But how could you live with yourself knowing that you are sleeping with Trevor? How could you look at Rochelle in the eye and have the guts to smile?'

Rutendo had always been Rochelle's best friend as they grew up. Their age difference had not stopped them from sneaking into each other's rooms and discuss their favourite topic, boyfriends. Naturally, the fact that Natsai was sleeping with Trevor would hurt Rutendo a lot. She, being her sister's friend was bound to tell her everything.

'That's none of your business, Rutendo. Both of you just seem to enjoy meddling in my business don't you?' Natsai eyed Rutendo with eyes full of pure venom. 'Anyway, do we have a deal? You don't say a word to Rochelle and I won't either.'

Rutendo looked torn between the two options. Running of to Rochelle was definitely tempting, but then she knew better than to piss Natsai.

She might have been the youngest and simple minded, but she sure knew how to cause trouble. She also knew how to manoeuvre her way out of tight spots. They hadn't nicknamed her the *devil's advocate* for no reason.

'Ok! We have a deal,' Rutendo said finally.

She wouldn't let a word of what she had done four years back slip to anyone.

Especially not Rochelle.

Unknown to either of them, in the shadows, Rosein had listened in on the whole conversation.

ZIMBABWE, HARARE
CHISHAWASHA HILLS, 1989

Feeling like a schoolboy on the first day of the holidays, Hugh sprang out of bed. Not since before his marriage had he woken in such good spirits. He had also never before been in quiet this same state of uncertainty as to the outcome of his pursuit of a female. *Would he be able to entice the beautiful Zanele Dube to bed? How conventional were South African women?* Had she really been interested in him, or was she toying with him for her momentary amusement?

It would not be long before he discovered the answer to such questions, he told himself, as he kissed Tracy's cheek and left the room.

When they met Zanele, she looked younger than her true age. 'I am so very pleased that you would come with me today,' Hugh said. 'I believe you will not feel your time has been wasted.'

This proved to be the perfect punishment for Tracy at the moment. *Why not?* She had denied him the gift of a child up to now. He found no fault in making a baby with a mistress. He was not sure if it had been true or Tracy's planning, but after her second miscarriage the doctor said she was not to get pregnant again. The doctor had said she would most probably die if we attempted. He had told her to cheer up for they at least had three beautiful daughters.

Such news hurt any normal couples, but he could see her wife's sigh of relief. He had met Zanele through a mutual friend. She had a different view on marriage from her wife. She adored children. She was warm and loving, the exact opposite of Tracy. Life always offered such a cruel irony.

ZIMBABWE, HARARE
CHISHAWASHA HILLS, 2016

Rosein had always known that something fishy was brewing right under everyone's nose. She had however assumed that it was something less offensive. She wasn't prepared for this drama. She would have enjoyed Rochelle's predicament had it not been for the fact that Trevor was cheating with Natsai. The idea was non-plausible, she felt nauseated.

Sleeping with your sister's husband was unforgivable. And here Rochelle was calling her a slut. How satiric. She remembered well that time years back when Rochelle had first distastes her. She had always assumed that Rosein had snatched Mandhla, Rochelle's high school sweetheart.

The cruel truth was that Mandhla had been fed up with Rochelle. He had detested Rochelle's bossy attitude. He had wanted a submissive girl, a girl who could be pushed around and look up to him. *Isn't it every man's dream?* A lady easy to sweep of her feet.

It was therefore natural that he had found Rochelle's ways unnerving. A very young girl who already believed in feminism. She was taking away his childhood, criticizing his book choices. According to her, a high school student was not supposed to resort to Mills and Boon, but rather to classics like Wuthering Heights, Sense and Sensibility, Romeo and Juliet and Pride and Prejudice.

It was then with pure gusto that he had resorted to the all too willing Rosein.

Back then, she had not known what true love was, but she had really liked the way he talked. Overly sweet and attentive. He had been smooth and understanding. She also liked the way his hungry eyes would appraise her, as if she was an ornamental piece.

ZIMBABWE, HARARE
CHISHAWASHA HILLS, 1990

It was not until Hugh returned home after a week away, ostensibly on a business trip, but in truth, enjoying himself enormously in Zaneles's house near Chishawasha Hills, that he learned of Vimbai's visit to his wife. The plan Tracy had made to be coldly angry with her husband went by the board when he presented himself in the kitchen in his best of moods.

His first thought as his wife launched into her tirade was that she had found out about Zanele. His relationship with Zanele had suddenly become interesting including that she had bore him a beautiful girl Rosein a few years back and as far as Hugh was concerned, it was thoroughly a novel experience to him. Zanele was proving a willing and magnificent teacher for he had suddenly discovered that he did not know much about females, and he had returned home that evening happy and congratulating himself for finding himself such a perfect mistress.

He was therefore in no mood for his wife's outbursts, but quite wittingly, he had managed to stay silent until he had realized that the mother of her son had visited and was sent packing by Tracy. He was beside himself with anger and disappointment.

'I have been searching for her for months now!' He said furiously. 'I want that boy, Tracy, and I intend to have him. You have no right to interfere.'

'And you had no right to keep me in ignorance of your intentions,' Tracy flared back, still too angry to be frightened by Hugh's uncustomary fury. 'I will not be humiliated in this way. It is outrageous!' She got no further, for Hugh caught her arm and held it in a vice like grip.

'I do not care. As far as the boy is concerned, I shall have him here. And I am also going to make myself his legal guardian. If you do not want that then too bad, go back to your parents' house. I hope that is understood.'

Tracy twisted free and turned away so that Hugh could not see the fear and fury in her eyes. She knew he did not love her, that he never had done so.

ZIMBABWE, HARARE
CHISHAWASHA HILLS, 2016

Rutendo couldn't have believed the sad truth if anyone would have told her.

She was struggling to believe her eyes. Her eyes stung and it felt like she was going to be really sick. Her head was hammering right at her temples.

Her mind was whirring at a terrific speed as she sank in the too soft rug under her feet. She had quickly drifted into a tormented sleep unknowingly.

It was Rosein who found her tossing and turning in her troubled sleep. Naturally, Rosein would have left her to her wits, but the way in which she was muttering Felix's name under her breathe made Rosein stop and help. Her face was bathed in snot and tears.

Rosein shook her sister gently. When she had finally awakened, she grabbed Rosein and cried like a baby trying to, but failing to explain the reason why she was in her current state. She was incoherent and Rosein could only make out the words, 'Felix,' and, 'How could he?'

It was then Rochelle walked in, Rutendo crying like a baby in Rosein's arms.

'What have you done to my sister?' Growled Rochelle, taking Rutendo from Rosein's care.

'Hey, Rochelle, would you at least please try to be nice?' Rosein said, exasperated.

'And why would I be nice to a prostitute?' Sneered Rochelle. Her attention was then drawn by

Rutendo's fresh sobs. Rutendo rested her head on Rochelle's chest and began to shake. With a softer tone than that, she had been using just seconds ago to Rosein she said, 'Who has done this to you my baby sister?'

After moments of hysterical sobbing and incoherent explanations, they at least got the gist of the story.

She had been cheated by Felix. She had walked in on him having sex with another person. Now she felt worthless and unwanted. She screamed and cursed flailing her arms all around the place. All the while, big fat tears rolling nonstop on her smooth cheeks.

Rochelle was frustrated. According to her, Felix had no right whatsoever to cheat on her sister. According to her, he had been lucky to get a lady like Rutendo and he should be thanking his gods that a person like Rutendo had accepted his marriage proposal. The beautiful and intelligent Rutendo, who would want to hurt such a loving soul? She cuddled her sister whispering words of encouragement.

Now Rochelle, an intelligent lawyer had found just the perfect solution to the incident. She was going to make Trevor take the case. Rutendo's divorce. She swore that with Trevor's expertise and ache for justice, Felix would not get even a dime off Rutendo. Because he, Felix, was being taken care of by Rutendo. All he had, it was from Rutendo. The car, the job and even his life.

As she tried to explain this to Rutendo, she cried even much more than the last time. This made Rochelle stop mid-sentence for a moment unsure whether her sister was normal or she now wanted professional help.

She would know the reason for Rutendo's weeping a minute later. Rutendo looked her in the eye, her face registering pain and whispered.

'When I said Felix cheated on me, I left out that it was Trevor with whom he was having sex.'

Rudo, their maid, was slight. Hugh was not sure whether she was timid or whether her halting English made her seem so. She had been with them only a month. The last house girl brought by Tracy's friend, was thickset and had arrived clutching a shangani bag. He was not there when Tracy looked through it. She did that routinely with domestic help because she wanted to know what was being brought into her home. He came when he heard Tracy shouting, in that impatient shrill manner she put on with domestic help to command authority.

The girl's bag was on the floor, open, clothes fluffing out. Tracy stood beside it, holding up, at the tips of her fingers, a skimpy looking short old dress.

'What is this for? You came to my house for prostitution?'

The girl looked down at first, silent, and then she looked at Tracy in the face and said quietly, 'I have no new fitting clothes Madam.'

Tracy's eyes bulged. She moved forward for a moment, as though to attack the girl in some way, and then stopped. 'Please carry your bag and go now!' She said.

The girl looked a little surprised before picking up her back and turning to the door. After she left, Tracy said, 'Can you believe that entire nonsense darling?'

'She doesn't have new clothes, she can't afford new clothes like you,' Hugh said.

Tracy stared at him. 'You feel sorry for her?'

He wanted to ask her, how she could not feel sorry for her? But the fear in her eyes silenced him. She was worried about a maid whom it would not occur to him to seduce.

Harare could do this to a woman married to a wealthy man. He knew how easy it was to slip into paranoia about many girls he worked with or maids. Still, he wished Tracy feared less.

She had, in the years since they married, grown a dislike of single women and a like for God. Before their marriage, she went to service once a week, a routine that she did because she had been brought up that way. After their wedding, she had switched to a new church. Later when he found out that her new church had a special prayer service for *Keeping Your Husband,* he had felt unsettled. Just as he had when he once asked her why her best friend from university, Liz, no longer visited them and Tracy said, 'She is still single.' As though that was a self-evident reason.

It had taken a fraction of a second for the message to sink into Rochelle. She desperately wanted to believe Rutendo, but she couldn't. She just couldn't.

Trevor, her own Trevor having sex with Felix? *How could it be? Was it possible that the same mouth she had kissed just that morning had also kissed Felix?* She felt sick and a heavy dizzying sensation as the thought that the manhood he had stocked into her vagina would have passed by Felix's rectum.

She felt repugnant.

'No. No, maybe there is just a simple explanation to all this confusion. Are you sure they were having sex as in, coitus?' Rochelle asked.

'Rochelle, I'm not a child okay? I know what I saw. I saw him, Trevor, sticking his penis up Trevor's rectum and... Oh God... Oh God...' Rutendo couldn't finish the sentence. She started to cry again. They both were crying. But Rochelle, being used to being the strong one was trying by all means to regain her composure so that she could comfort Rutendo.

'Rochelle, dear, you are in as much pain as Rutendo. Stop acting up and just let it all out. Let it all out.'

They had forgotten that Rosein was with them. She had been remarkably quiet throughout the drama. She hadn't seen were she could fit in into the ever weird life of number 12 Chishawasha Hills residents.

Rochelle surprised even Rosein by breaking down

in front of them. Rosein accompanied Rutendo to her room. She then prepared her a good cup of coffee to help calm her nerves. Rochelle had locked herself in her room and wouldn't let anyone, even their mother, in.

That, on its own, spoke volumes.

***

At their father's memorial day, they were all to dine together this was very difficult considering the most recent revelations. Despite the dirty business that had happened, they all felt mandated to honour their father. Therefore, they all dressed up and sat down for dinner.

Their mother didn't help the tension between the sisters at all because she had invited both Felix and Trevor insisting that they were family. Accidentally or by choice, Trevor sat between Natsai and Felix. He was also directly across Rochelle.

Their mother seemed to be oblivious of the tension that was building up every second as she continued to engage them in a polite conversation through dinner.

All hell had broken loose when Natsai attempted to apologize to Rochelle. Rochelle had completely lost her cool and ranted like a tigress, desperately trying to sink her claws into her sister.

Agitated, Natsai said something that changed everything. 'At least you have always known I was the bad one. What do you make of your beloved Rutendo who falsely accused you of being a lesbian only to stop you from partnering with Desiree Makumbe because apparently you would be getting more dough than her,' Natsai said.

Rochelle didn't want to believe Natsai, but it was the look on Rutendo's face that said it all. She had done it. She had stopped Rochelle from partnering with the most famous and successful lawyer in Zimbabwe all because of jealousy. The whole world seemed to be crushing in on her. The people she had loved and trusted for most of her adult life had screwed her. She felt alone and naked.

'How could you? I'm ashamed of you!' Their mother bellowed.

'Amai don't get carried away. All dirt is going down tonight. No more secrets,' Rutendo said putting on a dark smile, neither of them had seen her wear before. 'Listen guys,' she continued. 'How shocked I was to discover them two days ago, that our lovely mother here, the all respectable retired lawyer and elegant Tracy had a child with Felix's father. Spit it out mother, am I lying?'

The ongoing pandemonium ceased as eyes in the room rested on the old lady and Felix too. It was unthinkable that it would be even possible for her to cheat. *Or was it possible?*

Dirty secrets were being revealed.

Their mother's original name wasn't Tracy; she was Rumbidzai. She told them all about her initial marriage to Tafara, how she had had a child with Tafara, Felix before she had left for Cambridge where she had met their father Hugh.

Tracy argued that Hugh had had his own secrets.

Like how he had a son with a Vimbai and a daughter Rosein with a Zanele.

They had both discovered each other's secrets, but decided to set them apart. They had both agreed that it was better for the future of their law firm if they didn't split. Theirs had been a marriage of convenience after all.

'But mother, what kind of a sick game were you playing at?' Rutendo said furiously standing up when their mother had finished her narration. She stared at her and Felix, with disgust. 'Why would you let me marry your ex-husband's son? Oh God, it's more like I married my own brother and you just kept quiet about it. You had me sleeping with my brother, had kids with my brother?'

Her mother was about to reply, but Rutendo would not hear her reply as Felix beat her to it. To the sister's and Trevor's total shock, he didn't even look stunned or the bit worried.

'Don't be so naïve, Rutendo haven't you realized the conspiracy yet,' Felix said grinning.

According to Felix, Rumbidzai had found and approached him, telling him that she was his mother and told him that he marrying Rutendo had been no accident, that it had been her making. This was after Hugh had suddenly informed her that he wanted a divorce, and make his only son the heir to his empire leaving her with nothing.

Rumbidzai had approached Felix informing him that she was his mother, who had abandoned him all those years back, to his grandmother giving him up to the orphanage after she couldn't take care of him with his mother abroad. It had taken him some time to recover from the horror of him being married to his half-sister and having kids of incest, but as he was gay, he had quickly adapted when Rumbidzai had told him her plan. *To take over the whole of Truman and Truman Empire.*

Felix was to get a job at the firm. They would then try to overthrow Hugh from within. But it failed. When the plan had failed, she had then resorted to the obvious alternative after Hugh had discovered who Felix really was by accident. He had threatened to expose how so twisted Tracy's mind was, having her daughter marry her son and have kids. His last action.

The daughters were shocked when their mother finally confessed. She, Rumbidzai Tracy Dengu-Truman, had murdered their father, Hugh.